P9-CFE-183

OL' Lady Grizelda

Justin Matott

Illustrated by
John Woods Jr.

Clove Publications, Incorporated

Text copyright ©1998 by Justin Matott
Illustrations copyright ©1998 by John Woods
Book and text design by Herb Allison and Toby Balai

All rights reserved. No part of this publication may be reproduced
or transmitted in any form or by any means, electronic or mechanical,
including photocopy, recording, or any information storage and retrieval
system, without permission in writing from the publisher.

Requests for permission to make copies of any part of the work should
be mailed to Permissions Department, Clove Publications, Inc.
Box 261183 Littleton, CO 80163.

Library of Congress Cataloging-in-Publication Data
Matott, Justin
Ol' Lady Grizelda/written
by Justin Matott; illustrated by John Woods Jr. - 1st ed. p. cm.
Summary: an eccentric artist who lives on a hilltop over a township
is discovered by a curious young boy. A friendship is established
and prejudices are dwindled.
ISBN# 1-889191-09-4
{1. Old age-Fiction. 2. Artists-Fiction 3.} I. Woods, John Jr.,
1954-ill. II. Title

Second edition A B C D E

Printed in Korea

For JJ, Ethan, Garrett and Cee Cee
May the artist in you always flourish.
—J. M.

For Mama K,
who has never ceased to encourage me.
—J. W.

Special thanks to the third grade class of Mrs. Kathryn Kramer,
the fifth grade class of Ms. Paula Wills, and to the other children
of Cougar Run Elementary, Highlands Ranch, CO.

Then, there's Ol' Lady Grizelda, lives up on the hill,
mixing toenails and taters, which she boils in her still.
She works with a cauldron, mixing strange little brews,
from the hair and the claws, of her animal crews.
Though I've never been close up, she's hard to describe,
comes from somewhere else, must have been an odd tribe.
She's not really tall, and she's not really fat,
her nose is protruding, and her head's kind of flat.
Her hair is all tangled, and multi-colored too,
fixed up with pins, mud, and some kind of glue.
Ol' Lady Grizelda, some say mean, some say nice,
most don't really know her, no one's spoken to her twice.

Say they've seen her at midnight,
when out planting peas,
or she's looking for treasure,
without any keys.
Ol' Lady Grizelda,
looks all the day through,
for something she's lost,
without which she can't do.
She seems really lonely,
sits up there in a funk,
so many years spent,
"Just a'looking for junk."
She's singing 'bout treasure,
something she has misplaced,
sings about some lost rubies,
that one time her neck graced.
Have you looked in her garden,
at her really small graves?
With little white crosses,
maybe tunneling some caves.
Some tell of a time,
claimed treasure on her plot.
She's been looking for years,
'till she almost forgot.

Hear her breakfasts are weird, eggs of ostrich and muttons.
Boils her coffee, eats grounds, and chews on her buttons.
Ol' Lady Grizelda, seems she's really a loon.
She likes to eat kid stew, with a huge curvy spoon.

Ol' Lady Grizelda,
s'got a zoo full of beasts.
Newts, grizzlies and seals,
create her a fine feast.
Hear tell her ol' fridge's,
full of all sorts of odd things.
Snake tongues, lizards, potions,
marbles, worms and bat wings.

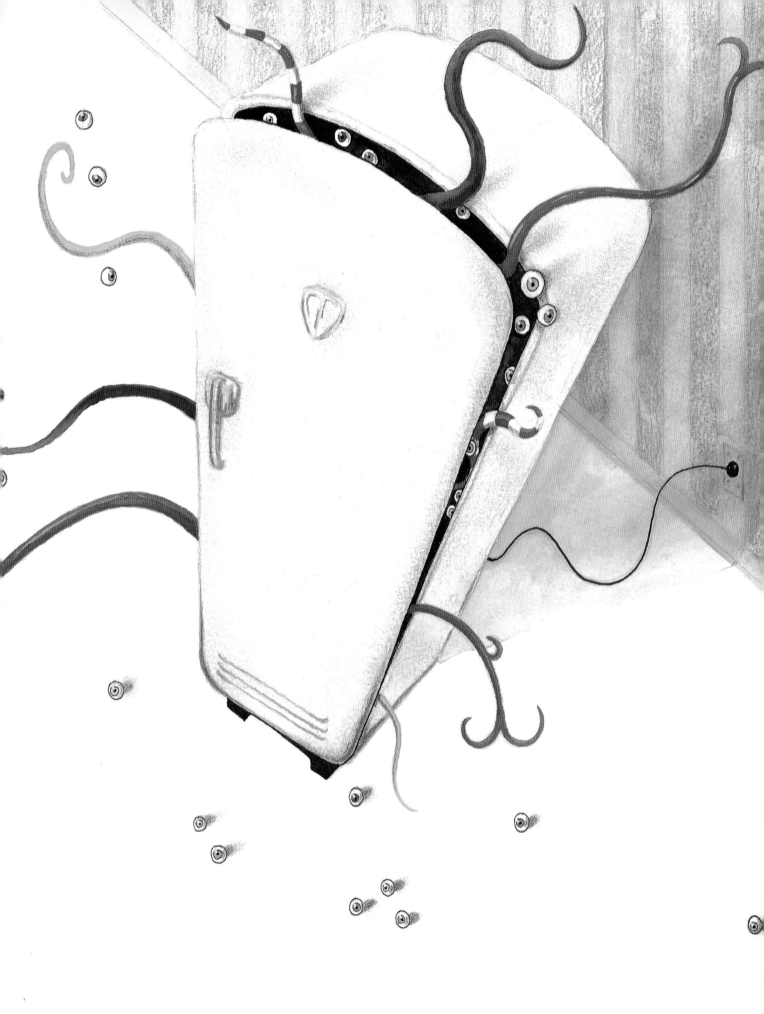

That lonely ol' lady,
plays all of the time.
Singing down in the canyon,
in an eerie, strange rhyme.
Have you heard when she wails,
to the clouds up above?
Hear tell she is sad,
something called a lost love.
Ol' Lady Grizelda,
all the night she does sing.

Voice carries down valleys,
with a strange sort of ring.
Notes line up in rows,
and fall down the cliff,
into the sea down below,
and from the waves get a lift.

When she's feeling frisky,
jumps off and floats down.

On the back of a fish,
she swims into town.

Ol' Lady Grizelda,
  always wandering about,
  with animals of all sorts,
  she sings loud and they shout!

She jogs and she skips,
  she seems to hold court,
  and along with her animals,
  she plays a weird sport.

Have you seen all those critters?
They're actually quite cute.
But I've never seen a rhino,
in a full three-piece suit.

Her only friends,
play dress up at night.
Walk up on the cliff-tops,
give townspeople a fright!

Ol' Lady Grizelda,
  she has caused quite a din.
  Spends time with her monsters,
  with fur, feathers and fin.

Have you seen her in daytime?
It's exceptionally rare.
She dances and prances,
in pink underwear.

She is loony! She's crazy!
She's a lonely ol' gal.
She's in need of a human,
or some kind of pal.

Have you seen her old car,

bounces noisy and loud.

Polishes it with a marmot,

she's really quite proud.

Ol' Lady Grizelda,
I knocked on her door.
She opened it widely,
and asked if there's more.
She knew I was coming,
saw me out by her fence.
She put on some tea,
let our talking commence.

Ol' Lady Grizelda,
  we sat out on her grass.
  Was a little past twilight,
  but in no time, time passed.
  The moon shining over
  her yard and her head,
  I didn't see anything,
  I needed to dread.
Ol' Lady Grizelda,
never went into town,
grew all of her food,
made the grocery man frown.
  So no one could know her,
  to this she seemed sad.
  She was afraid of them also,
  and that too was bad.
  Spoke more of the treasure,
  it had been there so long.
  She'd been digging and digging,
had come up with her song.
She cackled and laughed,
'till I thought she would burst.
  Then she pulled something out,
  from her little clutch purse.
  And then from her purse,
  dabbed on make-up a bit.
  She licked on her lip,
  and I swear, she DID spit!

I told her the rumors, about all the odd stories.

Told the ones about her, but I left out the gories.

She said "it's no matter," what folks said about things.

But she'd have to remember, to use more tone when she sings.

Ol' Lady Grizelda, she's both witty and quick,

recalled when it started, round the time of Saint Nick.

Seems they all came a'caroling, she was in a poor mood.

She grumbled and grimaced, showed them part of her brood.

She stood at the door, had a lizard and snake.

Shook them at the carolers, and made them all shake.

Since that dark, snowy night, the legend had grown,

'bout the little ol' lady, whom nobody had known.

Ol' Lady Grizelda, let the story commence,
'bout the time they all crossed her white, picket fence.
She drove them away with a whip and a chair.
All those stories about her, some just don't seem fair.
She sipped from her tea, went on to explain,
all the times that she's dug. She could take no more pain.
Her back's giving out, that's why she sings loud,
when she's digging out there, not meant to draw a crowd.
The little white crosses, just mark where she's been.
"I'm not burying anything!", she exclaimed with a grin.

We talked of the treasure,
  she would split with my crew.

"Full of rubies, that chest,
  and bars of gold, too."

It'd take more strong backs,
  to unearth from her map,

the treasure chest left there,
years ago by her Pap.

When she thought of her Dad,
tears rolled down her cheek.

And then she exclaimed,
"Hey maybe the creek!"

Her life's full of memories,
dreams of Greece, Rome and France.
Says she's seen all their paintings,
and that they love to dance.
She was born in the wrong time,
wish she could turn the clock back.
When things were so simple,
she'd live out of a pack.

"A gypsy" she said,
is what she'd like to be.
To hop trains and hop steamers,
then she could be free.
When she's painting or sculpting,
dreams both day and night,
of long distance places,
"But home is just right!"

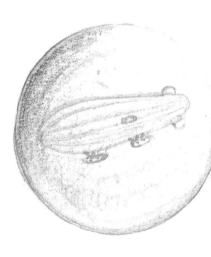

Ol' Lady Grizelda,
  paints flowers and things.
Wears paint on her skin,
  and many gold rings.
She paints under moonlight,
  makes sculptures of clay.
Says the whole world turns funny,
  but she likes it that way.
She stood in her kitchen,
  made me pudding and cream.
No monsters, no critters,
  and nobody screamed!!
A good time we had,
  we laughed and we dug.
Looked hard for her treasure,
  but found only a bug.

Ol' Lady Grizelda,
  found out her real name.
It isn't so crazy,
  it's really quite tame.
Her real name is Katy,
  short for Katherine or Kate.
Though she is sort of weird,
  she is totally great!

Convinced now she's harmless,
silly rumors and hearsay.
Folks misunderstood her,
just lives life her own way.
Grizelda's a sweetheart,
of this I am clear!
She's become my new granny,
No more reason to fear.
I'm going back tomorrow,
to help her pick peas.
You're welcome to join me,
we'll look for those keys.
Now here's where the story,
goes home round the bend.
I'm sorry it's over,
but this is THE END!

KATE